The Birds

DAPHNE DU MAURIER

Level 2

Retold by Derek Strange
Series Editors: Andy Hopkins and Jocelyn Potter

Introduction

Again and again the birds attacked him; their wings hit his eyes, their beaks cut into his hands and arms . . .

Nat, his wife and their two children live by the sea. Nat works on a farm. He loves watching the sea and the birds.

But this year something is different. The weather changes and suddenly it is very cold. There are more birds than last year. They are making a lot of noise. Nat feels afraid. But why? What is wrong?

The birds start to do strange things. Thousands and thousands of them fly over the farm. They are hungry and they are dangerous. Then the birds start to attack and kill.

Daphne du Maurier is a famous British writer. She was born in 1907 in London. Her mother and father worked in the theatre. She did not go to school but had lessons at home. She read many books and loved writing stories.

When Daphne Du Maurier was 19, she visited Cornwall in the south-west of England with her mother and sisters. She loved Cornwall, and she later made her home there. She found ideas for many of her exciting stories in Cornwall.

Her most famous books are *Jamaica Inn* (1936) and *Rebecca* (1938). She wrote many short stories too. Two of these are 'The Birds' (1952) and 'Don't Look Now' (1971). She died in her house in Cornwall in 1989 when she was eighty-one.

There are films of all these books and stories. Alfred Hitchcock made a famous film of *The Birds* in 1963. He changed some things in the story and moved it to America.

He sat near the sea and ate the food in his bag. He watched the birds.

The Birds

On the night of December the third the weather turned cold. Suddenly it was winter. The trees, red and yellow in their autumn colours one day, were suddenly brown and sad the next day.

Nat Hocken did not work at the farm all the time. He was older now and he only worked there for three days every week. They gave him the easier jobs now, too. He had a wife and children, but he best liked working out on the farm, quietly, with nobody to talk to, down near the beach with only the sea and the wind to listen to. He usually stopped work for half an hour at about twelve o'clock and sat near the sea and ate the food in his bag. He watched the birds. Autumn was the best time of the year for watching the birds, better than spring. In spring the birds moved away from the beach, but in autumn they came back, thousands and thousands of them, climbing and turning in the sky or coming down to stand for a few minutes near the water to find things to eat. Then they flew up into the wind again, above the cold, dark sea.

They never stopped. They were mostly seagulls, big white birds with black heads and hard yellow eyes. But there were other birds, too: big all-black birds from the farms behind the beach, with strong and dangerous yellow beaks; smaller brown or black or white fish-eating birds and farm birds, always moving, never quiet.

They waited for the sea to come up and go down. The sea left them new things to eat. They ran up and down together near the water and danced and screamed. Nat watched them and listened to them. Then suddenly they all flew up together into the wind,

1

and cried unhappily across the cold winter's sea and the open beach.

'Perhaps,' thought Nat, up there above the beach with his food, 'the wind tells the birds that it's autumn, that winter is coming? Perhaps they know that many of them are going to die in the cold months to come? But the birds are more excited than usual this year,' he thought. 'They're making more noise this year, crying and screaming more than last year or the year before that.' He watched the farmer at work up on the mountain behind the beach, with hundreds of white and black birds in the sky near him. 'And there are more birds here this year than last year, too,' he thought. 'There are always a lot of birds up on the mountain and near the farm buildings in autumn, but not these crowds of thousands and thousands of them. Why are there so many here this year?'

When he finished his day's work, Nat spoke to the farmer about the birds. 'Yes,' said the farmer, 'there are more birds here this year; I thought that, too. And some of them are not afraid of us. One or two of the seagulls came very near my head this morning – they nearly took my hat off! But I think the weather is going to turn; it's going to be a hard winter. That's why the birds are noisy and excited.'

Nat walked home slowly and watched the crowds of birds over the mountain in the west, in the orange light of the evening sun. There was no wind now and it was quite warm, but the farmer was right; that night the weather turned.

◆

Nat's bedroom looked east. At about two in the morning he suddenly heard the wind on the windows and on the roof of the house, an east wind, cold and hard. Nat listened, and he heard the noise of the angry sea on the beach. 'Why am I afraid?' he thought. 'Why am I afraid of the sea and the wind?' But he *was*

'One or two of the seagulls came very near my head this morning –
they nearly took my hat off!'

afraid. He moved nearer to his wife in the bed but he could not sleep. Then he heard a different sound at the window. He climbed out of bed and went to the window. He opened it and something flew past him, into the room. It cut his hand, then the thing – the bird, because it *was* a bird – flew out of the window again, away over the roof of the house, and the room was quiet.

There was blood on his hand. 'The bird was afraid, too,' he thought. He closed the window and went back to bed. He tried to sleep but he couldn't.

Some time later, there was a sound at the window again, stronger now. His wife turned in the bed and said, 'Look at the window, please, Nat. It's making a noise.'

'I looked at it twenty minutes ago,' he told her. 'There's a bird there. It wants to get in. Can you hear the wind? It's coming from the east and the birds know it's going to be cold outside.'

He opened the window a second time, and now there was not one bird but five or six of them. They flew into his face.

'They're attacking me!' he shouted and he hit at the birds with his arms. They flew out, over the roof and away. Quickly he closed the window.

'Did you see that?' he said. 'They attacked me. They tried to peck my eyes.' He stood near the window and looked out into the night but he could see nothing. His wife said something from the bed.

'I'm right,' he said. 'They were out there ready to attack me when I opened the window. They wanted to attack, not to come in.'

Suddenly there was a scream from the room where the children slept.

'It's Jill,' said his wife, and she quickly sat up in bed. 'Go to her, Nat. See what's wrong.'

'They're attacking me!' he shouted and he hit at the birds
with his arms.

He was outside the door of the children's bedroom when there was another scream. He opened the door and knew that there were birds in there. He could hear them and he could see them; their wings were on his face, in his hair, in front of his eyes. They flew in and out of the open window and they turned above the children in their beds.

'It's OK. I'm here,' he shouted. The birds flew at his face again and he hit at them. He pulled the children out of bed, pushed them out of the room and shut the door behind them. He was in the room with the birds now. He took a heavy book from the table next to Jill's bed and hit angrily at the birds again, left and right, right and left. Again and again they attacked him; their wings hit his eyes, their beaks cut into his hands and arms and there was blood down his face. He could not run to the door and open it; he did not want them to follow him into the other rooms of the house. Again and again he hit out at them with the book.

After a long fight in the dark room, the noise of the birds slowly stopped and he knew that there was light outside. It was nearly morning. He waited, listened; there was only the sound of the crying of one of the children, from the next room. The living birds were outside in the morning light, but on the floor of the room were the dead, nearly fifty of them. Nat looked at the dead birds. They were all small, mostly farm birds, friendly birds. Some of them now had blood, his blood, on their beaks.

He closed the window of the children's bedroom and went back to his wife. She was in bed with the two children. 'They're sleeping now,' she said quietly. 'But something cut Johnny near his eye, Nat. Jill says it was the birds. She says there were hundreds of birds in their room.'

'There are birds in there,' Nat said. 'They're dead now. I killed about fifty of them.' He sat down and took his wife's hand. 'It's

The living birds were outside in the morning light, but on the floor of the room were the dead, nearly fifty of them.

this weather. I don't think they're birds from round here; I think they came down from the north in this cold wind.' His face was tired.

'I'll go down and make a cup of tea,' he said.

After a cup of tea with his wife, things were better. He washed, put on his heavy work shoes and opened the back door. The children came down with his wife and they all had breakfast.

'They tried to peck us,' Jill said. 'They flew at Johnny's eyes.'

♦

The children finished their breakfast and Jill went to find her coat and school books. Nat said nothing, but his wife looked at him across the table and he knew what she wanted.

'I'll walk to the bus with her,' he said. 'I'm not working on the farm today.' And then more quietly, 'Close all the windows and doors today. Don't go outside.' Then he walked with Jill up the road, and waited with her and the other children for the bus to come. All the time he watched the sky and the trees but he didn't see any birds. There weren't any birds there. Everything was quiet.

After the bus went, he saw Mrs Trigg, the farmer's wife, and they talked about the weather. 'Where is this cold weather coming from?' she asked. 'Is it Russia, do you think? The radio says that it's going to get worse, too, you know.'

'We didn't listen to the radio this morning,' Nat said. He tried to tell her about his fight with the birds in the children's room in the night, but he saw that she thought is was only a story. She wasn't interested. He walked home.

He went up to the children's room and put all the dead birds into a bag. Yes, there were fifty of them. He took the bag of dead birds down to the beach and threw them out into the sea, but the wind took them and carried them away along the beach.

'They're flying again!' he thought suddenly. 'They're not dead!' He knew that they *were* dead, but he was afraid.

He stood and watched the angry green and white of the sea for a minute, and listened to the crying of the wind.

Then he saw them. Seagulls. Out there on the water.

First he thought they were white, breaking water, but then he saw that they were seagulls. Hundreds, thousands, tens of thousands of them, sitting on the water, waiting. East and west, as far as he could see, there were seagulls out there on the water.

He turned and started quickly for home. 'I must tell some-body,' he thought. 'Somebody must know.' But what could anybody do?

He came near the house and his wife opened the door, excited. 'Nat, it's on the radio. About the birds. It's not only here, it's all over the country. Something is happening to the birds. They're crowding into the towns and trying to get into people's houses, thousands of them. And they're attacking people in the streets. They say the birds are all hungry with this cold weather, you see. They say we must close all the doors and windows, and children must stay inside.'

Nat was excited. 'I knew it. Something is happening to the birds! I was right,' he said. 'And down at the beach I saw thousands of seagulls out there on the sea. They're waiting.'

'What are they waiting for?'

'I don't know,' he said slowly. 'But I'm going to put wood over all our windows and doors this morning. I think it's important to do what the radio says.'

'You think they're going to attack, try to break down our windows and doors when they're closed? How can they?'

Nat did not answer. He remembered those thousands and thousands of gulls out there on the sea. Big, strong birds with hard yellow eyes and dangerous beaks.

He worked all morning, putting up wood over the windows and doors of the house.

'Lunch is ready,' his wife called from the kitchen, and he went down. He was happy with his morning's work. They listened to the radio again at one o'clock and heard about the crowds of birds in London, on all the roofs and windows and trees. He turned off the radio and got up to start work on the kitchen windows.

'Wood on the windows down here, too?' his wife asked.

'Yes. Better, I think,' he said. 'How much food have we got in the house?'

'I'm going shopping tomorrow, you know that.'

Nat did not want her to be afraid so he said nothing, but he thought, 'I don't think she's going to town tomorrow,' and he went to look in the kitchen cupboard where the tins of food were. There were five or six tins and a little bread. They had food for about two days.

Later in the afternoon he went outside and looked at the sea. The gulls were not on the water now, they were up in the sky, thousands of them climbing and turning, but quietly, without a sound.

He turned and ran back to the house. 'I'm going for Jill,' he said, and took his coat and started walking up the road to the bus-stop. Again and again he looked behind him and above him, but there was nothing there. Out over the sea the gulls flew up and up, round and round.

He was half an hour early at the bus-stop. In that half-hour something black moved slowly up across the sky from the sea. There were thousands of birds flying together to the east and north, south and west.

'They're going for the towns,' he thought. 'They're not interested in us. The gulls are waiting for us.'

The bus came slowly up the road. Jill climbed out with three

He worked all morning, putting up wood over the windows and doors of the house.

or four other children. The bus went on to the town. He told the other children to run home as fast as they could, not to stop and play in the road.

He could see the gulls now, coming up from the sea, across the beach, without a sound. Quiet.

'OK, let's go now,' he said to Jill.

'Look, Dad. Look at the gulls. Where are they flying to? What are they all doing?'

He took her hand and pulled her down the road, afraid again now.

'Do you want me to carry you, Jill? Here, come on, up on my back.' But Jill was heavy and they went slowly. She started to cry; she could see that he was afraid. He put her down again and they started running down the road, hand in hand.

At the farm they saw the farmer in his car. Nat called to him, 'Can you take Jill with you?'

A smile came to Mr Trigg's happy, round face. 'It's going to be interesting, you know,' he said. 'All these birds. I'm going out with my gun to kill some of them. Want to come? I've got another gun.'

Nat did not want to talk in front of Jill. 'I don't want a gun, thanks, but can you take young Jill home for me? She's afraid of the birds. I'll walk home.'

Jill climbed in and the car moved away. Nat walked and watched the sky. The gulls were quite near the farm now.

'They're going to attack the farm,' he thought.

He walked faster. The farmer's car stopped at his house, turned and came back up the road. It stopped and Nat talked to Mr Trigg for a minute or two.

'Have you got wood over your windows?' he asked the farmer.

The farmer laughed. 'Wood over the windows? No! That's radio talk, that's all. I've got more important things to do than

'Look, Dad. Look at the gulls. Where are they flying to?
What are they all doing?'

putting wood over my windows. The birds can't get in with the windows closed, you know.' He smiled. 'See you in the morning,' he called and he drove on up the road to the farm.

Nat walked on quickly. He watched the roofs of the farm buildings and the trees carefully. Suddenly he heard the sound of wings behind him. A black-headed gull attacked from behind, flew past his ear and tried to peck at him. It turned and flew up, ready to attack again. There were other gulls there now, too. Nat put his arms up over his head and ran to the door of their house. The birds attacked again and again, without a sound, cutting into him with their beaks. The only thing he could hear before they attacked was the sound of their wings. There was blood on his hands and arms but they did not get his eyes.

He found the door and shouted. 'It's me! Nat! Open the door! Quick!'

He saw a big seagull up in the sky above him, ready to attack, ready to break open his head with its long yellow beak, now red with his blood. It pulled its wings in, pushed out its beak in front of it, and down it came at his head. Nat screamed, and the door opened. He jumped inside and the gull hit the door behind him, breaking the wood.

The cuts on his face and arms were not bad. His hands were the worst.

The children started to cry when they saw the blood on him.

'It's OK now,' he said. 'It's nothing too bad. Go and play with Johnny in the other room now, Jill. Mum's going to wash these cuts for me.'

His wife washed the blood off his face and arms. Her face was white. 'I saw them in the sky when Jill arrived with Mr Trigg,' she said. 'Then I closed the door fast, but I couldn't open it again when I heard you outside.'

'Thank God it was only me out there, not Jill too,' he said. 'They're flying in from the sea, going for the towns. I saw them

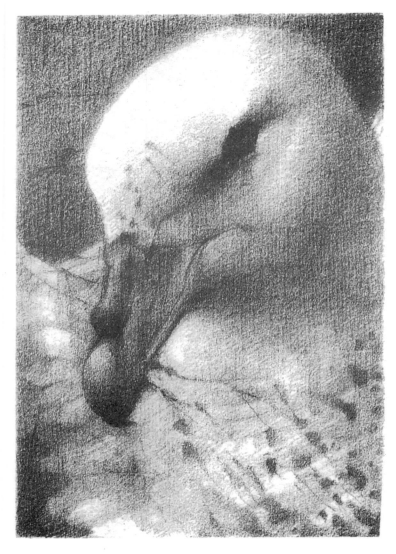

It pulled its wings in, pushed out its beak in front of it, and down it came at his head.

He found more wood and old tins and he put them up over the inside of the windows too.

from the bus-stop, thousands of them. They're going to attack there, too, anything or anybody out in the streets. And nobody is ready for them. Let's listen to the radio again at six o'clock.'

They went through to the children in the other room. Jill was sitting on a chair, white and afraid, but Johnny had a small red car and he was happy with it on the floor.

'I can hear the birds, Dad,' Jill said. 'Listen.'

Nat listened. Noises came from the windows, from the door. The wings and beaks of hundreds of birds trying to get in. 'They want to kill us,' he thought.

But he said, 'It's OK. We've got wood over all the windows, Jill. The birds can't get in.'

He went to look at the windows. His work was good: there were no places where the birds could get in. But he found more wood and old tins and he put them up over the inside of the windows, too. He could hear the birds outside all the time.

'Turn on the radio,' he said. 'Let's listen to something.'

With the radio on, the children could not hear the noise of the birds. He went up to the bedrooms and put more wood on the inside of the windows there, too. He heard the birds on the roof, scratching with their feet and pecking with their beaks.

'We must sleep down in the kitchen tonight,' he thought. 'Make a fire and sleep on the floor. It's too easy for the birds to get in up here.'

He started to bring their beds down to the kitchen and his wife watched him, her eyes dark and afraid.

'Are they up in the bedrooms, Nat?' she asked quietly.

'No. We're OK.' He smiled at her. 'We're all going to sleep together in the kitchen tonight, that's all. It's warmer down here near the fire. Then those birds can't stop us sleeping, with their noise at the windows.'

17

The children helped him to push the table and chairs away from the fire. He moved the table across the door. 'That's good,' he thought. 'We're going to be OK in here with the fire, and we've got food for two days, perhaps three. After that . . .'

He didn't want to think about it now. 'We can listen to the radio and think about what to do later,' he thought.

At six o'clock they listened to the radio again. A man spoke, quietly and unhappily now, different from the man on the radio at lunchtime.

'Thousands of birds are attacking anybody they see . . . They are also attacking buildings . . . The police cannot help . . . Everybody must stay inside tonight and stay together . . . Do not go out on the streets . . . Close all doors and windows.'

Then there was nothing. The radio stopped early that night. Nat turned it off. He looked at his wife and she looked back at him, white-faced.

'There's no more radio tonight,' he told the children.

'Is it the birds?' asked Jill. 'Are the birds doing it, Dad?'

'I don't know,' Nat answered. 'But we're OK without the radio for one evening.'

They tried to talk and then they sang together for five or ten minutes, but all the time they could hear the sound of small hard feet scratching on the roof, wings at the windows and beaks pecking at the doors.

'Let's have our dinner early tonight. I'm hungry,' said Nat. He tried to smile. 'Ask Mum. Something good, eh, Mum? Something we all like?'

His wife put a smile on her face and started to make their dinner. Nat helped her and made a lot of noise, singing and talking and laughing. The noise of the birds was not so bad then. He went up to the bedrooms for a minute and listened. There was no sound of the birds on the roof now.

At six o'clock, they listened to the radio again. A man spoke,
quietly and unhappily now.

'They're clever. They know they can't get in here. They're trying other places,' he thought.

They had a good dinner, washed the plates and glasses and put them away in the cupboard. They thought that they heard aeroplanes at one time but then the sound died away.

'Are the aeroplanes coming to help us, Dad?' Jill asked.

'No, they're going to London, I think,' said Nat. 'Come on now, time for bed.'

His wife helped the children to get ready for bed and he went round the house again and looked at all the windows and doors. He thought about those important people in London, all trying to find an answer to this attack by the birds. 'They're working on it now,' he thought, 'but I don't see what they can do. Aeroplanes aren't going to help much. This isn't a job for aeroplanes or guns.'

♦

Everything was quiet up in the bedrooms. No more scratching at the roof or pecking at the wood over the windows. The wind was strong; he could hear it under the roof and he could hear the sea breaking down on the beach.

'It's the sea,' he thought suddenly. 'The birds come and go with the sea; they follow it up and down, in and out. They attack when the sea is in and they go back to the water and the beach when it's out. That's why they aren't here now. The sea is out.' He looked at his watch. 'Nearly eight o'clock. So we've got six hours without attack. When the sea comes in again, at about half past one in the morning, the birds are going to attack.'

First, he and his wife and children must sleep for three or four hours, up to about midnight. 'Then,' he thought, 'I must go up to the farm and see that they're OK up there.'

He called quietly to his wife and she came up. 'I'm going out later, after some sleep,' he told her.

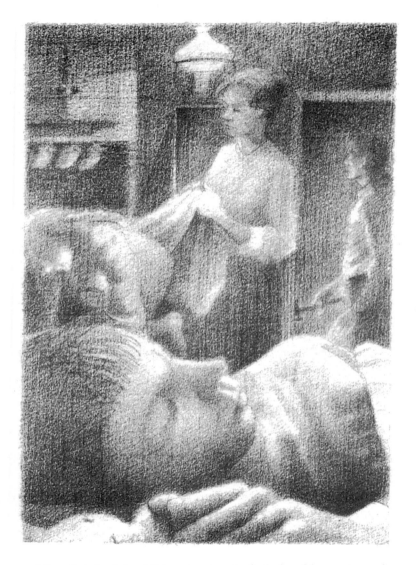

His wife helped the children to get ready for bed and he went round the house again and looked at all the windows and doors.

'I don't want you to go, Nat. I don't want you to leave us here,' she said. 'Please don't go. Please, Nat.'

'OK, love, OK. I can wait for morning and we can listen to the radio again then too, at seven. But in the morning, when the sea goes out again, I'm going up to the farm. I want to get some more bread from Mrs Trigg, and perhaps some milk and vegetables.'

He thought of the smiling, laughing farmer, Mr Trigg, in his car with his guns, with more important things to do than putting wood over the windows of his house. Perhaps the birds were inside the Triggs' house now. Nat went quietly down to the kitchen.

The children were in bed. His wife sat near them on a chair. She watched him.

'What are you going to do?' she asked quietly.

He put one finger to his mouth, for quiet, and went to the back door. Very carefully he opened it and looked outside.

It was very dark. The wind was stronger now, and very cold, from the sea. Outside the door were hundreds of dead birds, under the windows, in the garden. Dead from their attacks on the house. He kicked them away from the door with one foot. There were no living birds out there. The living were out on the sea again now, sitting on the water, waiting for the next attack. Only the dead were here.

He went back into the house, closed the door and put the table across it again. There was blood from the dead birds all over his shoes and there was some on his hands, too. He washed his hands carefully.

His wife made him a cup of tea and he drank it thirstily. He was very tired.

'It's going to be OK,' he said, and smiled at his wife. 'We're getting through.'

On his bed, he closed his eyes and slept. But into his sleep

Outside the door were hundreds of dead birds, under the windows,
in the garden.

came pictures of flying black wings and rivers of blood . . . and something he must get up and do. What was it? In his sleep, he could not think what it was. He had another important job to do and he must not forget it, but what was it? He opened his eyes and saw his wife's white face above him in the dark, crying and afraid.

'They're back,' she said. 'They're starting again.'

He listened and heard the scratching on the roof and the wings on the windows again. He looked at the fire and saw a black, dead bird on it. Then he remembered the thing he must do, the important job. The fire! He must build up the fire again!

'Quick!' he said. 'The fire. I forgot it last night. Put some more wood on the fire!'

He jumped out of bed and started to put wood on the fire. No more birds could fly down there. Soon they started to hit their wings more and more angrily on the windows and began pecking more angrily at the doors. But they could not get in.

He thanked God that they had an old house with thick, strong doors and small windows. 'The birds can break their beaks and wings on those,' he thought, 'they can die trying to get in here, but they can't get us.'

He looked quickly at his watch. Three o'clock. More than four hours before the sea turned – at about quarter to eight in the morning, he thought – and started to go out again. More than four hours before the birds stopped their attack and went back to the sea.

'Make the children some hot milk, love,' he said to his wife, 'and let's have a cup of tea. We can't sit here and do nothing.' That was the best thing to do: move about, talk, eat, drink, stop his wife and the children from thinking about the birds.

'Come on now, Jill. Bring me some more wood for the fire. We must have a good fire all the time to stop those old birds from

He opened his eyes and saw his wife's white face above him in the dark, crying and afraid.

coming in. I must get some more wood from the farm when I go up there in the morning. I can go out when the birds aren't here, when the sea is out.'

They drank tea and hot milk and ate some bread and butter. There was not much bread now, Nat thought.

'Stop it!' shouted Johnny at the windows. 'Stop that noise, you dirty old birds.'

'That's right,' said Nat, and smiled at his son. 'We don't want those old birds here.'

They began to laugh every time they heard birds breaking their beaks or wings on the wood outside the windows and doors.

'Listen! There he goes!' Jill shouted. 'He's dead!' And they all laughed again.

This was the thing to do, fight back, laugh at the birds, shout at them. They could get through the night together and then listen to the first news on the radio in the morning.

'Give me a cigarette,' he said to his wife. 'A good smoke helps me to forget about those birds.'

'There are only two here,' she said. 'I wanted to get you some more from the shop.'

'Leave one in there for later, love,' he said.

The children did not want to go back to sleep now. They couldn't sleep with all the noise on the roof and windows and the scratching at the doors. He sat on one of the beds with one arm round his wife and the other round Jill. Johnny sat in his mother's arms, warm and unafraid.

'They don't get tired of this game,' Nat said 'They come back again and again.'

◆

The noise of the beaks and feet and wings went on and on for hours. Suddenly, in all the other noise, Nat heard a new sound. It

26

'Stop it!' shouted Johnny at the windows. 'Stop that noise, you dirty old birds.'

was a harder attack by a stronger beak than the others out there. It broke one of the windows and cut into the wood over one of the doors. Nat tried to think what bird this was, this new, bigger, more dangerous attacker. He heard strong feet pulling at the roof and he knew what bird this was: it was one of the hunting birds.

'Three hours before the sea turns and the birds stop,' he thought. 'Hunting birds now. Killers. What can I do?' He went up to the bedrooms and stood and listened outside the closed doors. There was a quiet noise from inside the children's room. There were birds in there. He put his ear to the door. No mistake. He could hear the sounds of birds' feet on the floor and their wings on the inside of the door. No sound came from the other bedroom. He went into it and began to bring out chairs and other things to take down to the kitchen.

'Come down, Nat, what are you doing?' called his wife.

'In a minute,' he shouted. 'I'm putting some more things across the bedroom doors.'

He did not want her to come up; he did not want her to hear the birds' feet on the floor and the sound of their wings on the inside of the bedroom door.

At five-thirty they had an early breakfast. Nat wanted to give his wife something to do, to stop her from thinking too much about their attackers. And he did not want her to know about the birds up in the children's room. It was lucky that that bedroom was not over the kitchen; she could not hear the scratching of the birds up there.

He looked at his watch again and again. The hands moved round slowly. 'They must stop when the sea turns,' he thought, 'they must or they're going to break through before I can put more wood over the windows and doors. They can't go on and on without stopping, without food, without . . .' There were so many things to think about, so many things to do before the next attack, to be ready. And he wanted to sleep.

He heard strong feet pulling at the roof and he knew what bird this was: it was one of the hunting birds.

'Perhaps it's better in the towns? Perhaps I can telephone from the farm and we can get a car and drive to my brother's place . . .'

His wife started talking and he forgot about sleep and cars and driving into the town.

'What? What is it?' he said.

'The radio,' she said. 'It's nearly seven. Let's listen to the radio.'

They turned on the radio and waited. His watch showed seven o'clock, but not a sound came from the radio. Nothing. They waited for a quarter of an hour, but there was nothing. Nothing came through.

'Perhaps they said eight o'clock,' he said.

They left the radio on.

'It's getting light outside,' his wife said. 'And the birds aren't making all that noise now. Listen.'

She was right. The pecking and pulling and scratching sounds were weaker now. There were not so many birds on the roof.

'The sea's turning; it's going out,' he said.

By eight o'clock there were no birds outside. Everything was quiet again. Only the wind made a noise. The children slept. At half past eight Nat turned the radio off.

'What are you doing, Nat? We want to hear what they say, what's happening with these birds all over the country,' said his wife.

'They aren't going to tell us anything, love. There isn't going to be anybody on the radio today,' Nat answered.

He went to the door and slowly pulled back the table and chairs across it. He opened it carefully and kicked away the hundreds of dead birds outside. He had six hours before the birds came back and he knew that he must work hard. Food, wood for the fire and milk for the children were the most important things. They must be ready for the next attacks that afternoon and the next night.

*Everything was quiet again. The children slept. At half past eight
Nat turned the radio off.*

He went out into the garden. There were the living birds, outside the house. They didn't attack him; they stood. The gulls were out on the sea again, but these farm birds waited there in the garden, outside in the road, on the trees. Lines and lines of them, they watched him quietly and did nothing. He walked carefully down the small garden. The birds did not move.

'I must get some food,' Nat said, 'I must go to the farm and get some food.'

He went back to the house. He went round it and looked at all the windows and the doors. He went up and opened the door to the children's bedroom. There were no living birds in there but there were dead birds all over the floor. He went down to the kitchen again.

'I'm going to the farm,' he said.

His wife did not want him to go. 'I saw the living birds out there in the garden, Nat. Please take us with you. We can't stay here without you.'

He thought for a minute. 'OK. Come on then. Let's go,' he said. 'Bring some bags. We can put everything in them.'

They put on warm coats – the north wind was deadly cold – and Nat took Jill's hand.

'The birds,' she cried quietly, 'I don't like the birds out there, Dad.'

'They're not going to attack us,' he said, 'not in the day.'

Very slowly and quietly they started walking along the road, up to the farm. The birds did not move. They waited, their heads turned into the wind.

◆

When they arrived at the farm, Nat stopped and told his wife to wait with the two children.

'But I want to see Mrs Trigg,' she said. 'There are a lot of things to ask her for, not only bread, but . . .'

'Wait here,' Nat said. 'I'm coming back in a minute.'

No smoke came from the house. He was afraid. He did not want his wife or the children to go into the farm.

'Do what I say, please,' said Nat.

She pulled Jill and Johnny under a tree out of the wind and he went into the farm without them. He saw the car in front of the house, not in the garage. There was no glass in any of the windows of the house and there were hundreds of dead gulls near the front door. There was a crowd of living birds on the roof and on the trees round the house. They did not move. They watched him.

Jim, the farm boy, was near the car. Dead, his face cut and bloody, his gun near him. The front door was closed but Nat easily climbed through a window next to it. Mr Trigg was on the floor near the telephone. Dead too, with blood all over his face and his eyes pecked out.

'Perhaps he was on the phone to the police or somebody when the birds came for him,' Nat thought. He could not see or hear Mrs Trigg. 'Perhaps she's up in one of the bedrooms?' he thought, but he knew that she was dead too. 'Thank God there were no children.'

He started to go up to the bedrooms but stopped and turned back, nearly screaming, nearly ill, when he saw Mrs Trigg's legs on the floor in one of the open doors up there. Near her on the floor were dead black-headed gulls.

'It's no good,' thought Nat. 'I can't do anything to help them now. I've only got five hours. I must take everything I can find in the house and get out.'

He went back to his wife and the children. 'I'm going to put the things into the car. We can take it home and come back for more later,' he said.

'Where are the Triggs?' asked his wife.

'They aren't there. Perhaps they're with friends,' he said. 'I'm

He stopped and turned back, nearly screaming, nearly ill, when he saw Mrs Trigg's legs on the floor in one of the open doors.

going to get the car. You can sit in it and wait. Don't come into the house; there are hundreds of dead birds in there.'

Her eyes watched him all the time. He knew that she understood. She didn't ask to help him again; she waited quietly in the car with the children.

They went back to the farm three times before they had everything they wanted. He took more wood for the windows, wood for the fire, some bread, tins of vegetables and fruit, milk and much more.

The last time he stopped near the bus-stop and got out of the car. He went over to the telephone box. Nothing; no answer. The telephone line was dead. He looked out across the farm, down to the sea and across to the mountain, but nothing moved, everything was quiet. Only the waiting, watching birds, some of them sleeping with their beaks under their wings, getting ready for the next attack.

'They're not eating,' he thought, 'only standing or sleeping. Why?' Then he remembered. 'They ate in the night. They ate all they wanted. That's why they aren't moving this morning . . .' He went quickly back to the car and got in.

'Go quickly past that tree,' his wife said quietly. 'There's a dead man in the road there and I don't want Jill to see.'

It was quarter to one when they arrived back at the house. Only one more hour before the birds began again.

'I'm not going to eat now,' he said. 'I must put all these things away and then do some work on the windows and doors.'

He got everything inside the house and started work on the windows. He went carefully round the house, looking at every window and door. He climbed up on the roof too and looked out to sea. Something moved out there. Something white and black on the cold dark green of the sea. A ship? Was it a ship?

He waited, his eyes watering in the cold wind, looking out to sea. He was wrong; it was not ships. It was the gulls. Slowly, wing

He climbed up on the roof too and looked out to sea. Something
moved out there. A ship? Was it a ship?

to wing, they left the water and flew up into the sky, turning, turning, up and up.

'The sea is coming in again,' he thought. 'Time for the next attack.'

He climbed down and went into the kitchen. The family were at lunch. It was after two o'clock. He closed the front door and pushed the table in front of it again.

His wife had the radio on again. No sound came from it. 'I can't get anything on it,' she said. 'All the stations are dead.'

'Perhaps it's the same all over the world,' he said.

She gave him a plate of the Triggs' soup and some of the Triggs' bread and butter.

They ate without saying anything, thinking. Then the noise of the birds started again. Small hard feet scratching at the roof, wings pushing at the windows, gulls' beaks pecking at the wood.

'Is America going to helps us?' asked his wife. 'They helped us before; they were our friends. Perhaps they're going to help us again this time?'

Nat did not answer. They had food and firewood for the next three or four days here in the house, in boxes in the corner of the kitchen. After lunch he wanted to put everything away in the cupboards.

'At quarter to nine, when the sea starts to go out again and everything is quiet, we can put the children to bed and get some sleep,' he said, 'before they start again at three in the morning.'

The smaller birds were at the windows now. He could hear the light noise of their beaks on the wood and the quiet sound of their wings. The big hunting birds and the seagulls did not go for the windows; they attacked the wood of the door. Nat listened to the angry sound of the beaks cutting into the new wood.

'I'm going to smoke that last cigarette now, I think,' he said to his wife.

'I'm going to smoke that last cigarette now, I think,' he said to his wife. 'I forgot to get some more from the farm this morning.'

He laughed and took out the last cigarette.

ACTIVITIES

Pages 1–8

Before you read

1 Look at the Word List at the back of the book. Put these words in the right places.

   beak   pecked   screamed   seagull   wings

   The **a** ..... stood on the beach. It **b** ..... at the dead fish with its long yellow **c** ..... Then it **d** ..... loudly. It opened its **e** ..... and flew into the sky.

   attacked   blood   crowd   fight   scratched

   The cat **f** ..... the dog. It **g** ..... the dog's nose. There was **h** ..... everywhere. A **i** ..... of people watched. Then someone stopped the **j** ..... .

2 Read the Introduction to this book. Answer these questions.

   a What happens to the weather?

   b What is different about the birds?

   c Where did Daphne du Maurier find ideas for her stories?

3 Discuss these questions.

   a Do you like birds or are you afraid of them?

   b Can a bird hurt a person? How?

While you read

4 Underline the right words in *italics*.

   a Every year the birds leave the beach in the *autumn / spring*.

   b When the sea *comes up / goes down*, the seagulls can find food on the beach.

   c The farmer thinks *the weather is / the birds are* going to change.

   d Nat can't sleep because of the *birds / wind* at the window.

   e *The children fight / Nat fights* the birds in the bedroom.

   f The birds in the children's room are *seagulls / farm birds*.

   g Nat kills *fifty / hundreds* of birds.

41

After you read

5 Nat is in the children's room. He is fighting the birds. Answer these questions.
   a Is it hot or cold? Why?
   b Is it light or dark? Why?
   c There is a lot of noise. What are the sounds?
   d How do the birds attack Nat?
   e How does Nat feel, do you think?

6 Work with another student. You live in the village near Nat Hocken's. Last night the birds attacked your houses too. Today everything is quiet. Talk about it. What is happening? Why?

Pages 8–14

Before you read

7 Which of these things will happen, do you think?
   a The birds will come back tonight.
   b The birds will get into all the rooms in the house.
   c The birds will kill one of the Hockens.

While you read

8 Tick (✓) the things that Nat does.
   a He takes Jill to the school bus. .....
   b He tells Mrs Trigg about his fight with the birds. .....
   c He tells his wife about the birds in the towns. .....
   d He tells her about all the birds on the sea. .....
   e He puts wood over the doors and windows. .....
   f He says to his wife, 'You can't go shopping tomorrow.' .....
   g He carries Jill all the way to the house. .....
   h He runs into the house before the big seagull hurts him. .....

After you read

9 What does the radio say? Make sentences with these words.

    a to be   is going   worse   the weather

    b into cities   all over the country   are crowding   the birds

    c in the streets   they   people   are attacking

    d must   doors and windows   people   their   close

    e inside   must   children   stay

Pages 14–20

Before you read

10 Work with another student. Have this conversation.

Mr and Mrs Trigg don't think the birds are a problem. They talk and laugh about them at dinner that evening.

While you read

11 <u>Underline</u> the mistake in each sentence. Write the right words.

    a Johnny is white and afraid.   ....

    b They can hear the birds when the radio is on.   ....

    c They have food for a week.   ....

    d They sing because they want to hear the birds.   ....

    e Nat makes the dinner.   ....

    f The important people in London are not thinking about the problem of the birds.   ....

After you read

12 You are in the Hockens' house. Which of these things make you most afraid? Number them 1 to 6 (6 is the worst).

..... the radio stops

..... the birds scratch and peck at the windows and doors

..... you can't see out because of the wood over the windows

..... you don't have much food

..... you have to sleep in the kitchen

..... you hear aeroplanes in the sky

Pages 20–26

Before you read

13 Nat says, 'This isn't a job for aeroplanes or guns.' What can people do about the birds? Talk to other students. Who has the best idea?

While you read

14 Finish the sentences on the left with words from the right.

a The birds attack	**h** the fire.
b Nat wants to get	**i** old and strong.
c When Nat wakes up, ...	**j** and wait for eight o'clock.
d He forgot to build up	**k** at the birds.
e Their house is	**l** food from the farm.
f They laugh and shout	**m** when the sea comes in.
g They sit together on the bed	**n** the birds are back.

After you read

15 Answer these questions.
   a Why do the family sleep when the sea is out?
   b When Nat goes outside, why does he find only dead birds?
   c Nat says, 'We're getting through.' What does he mean?
   d In his sleep, Nat remembers an important job. What is it?
   e Nat and his wife don't want the children to think about the birds. So what do they do?

Pages 26–32

Before you read

16 Discuss these questions.
   a Can things get worse for the Hocken family? How?
   b Will help come? Who or where from?
   c Nat says, 'They don't get tired of this game.' Do you think the birds will get tired of it?

17 Are these sentences right (✓) or wrong (✗)?

   a There are now big, strong hunting birds with the
     seagulls and farm birds. .....

   b Hunting birds are not as dangerous as seagulls. .....

   c The birds are inside the two bedrooms. .....

   d The birds attack for hours and don't stop for food. .....

   e At seven o'clock the birds are quieter. .....

   f Nobody is talking on the radio. .....

   g Nat's wife doesn't want to go to the Triggs' farm. .....

After you read

18 You are with the Hockens. You can bring three things back from
the Triggs' farm. What will you bring?

Pages 32–end

Before you read

19 Mr and Mrs Trigg didn't put wood over their doors and windows
last night. Nat and his family are going to the Triggs' farm. What
will they find there, do you think?

While you read

20 Read the sentences. Put these words in the right places.

   America   cigarette   dead   hungry   ill   people   ship

   a The .... at the Triggs' farm are all dead.

   b Nat feels .... when he sees Mrs Trigg.

   c The telephone lines are ....

   d The birds aren't .... because they ate people in the
     night.

   e Nat thinks he sees a .... but it's really the seagulls.

   f Nat's wife hopes that .... can help them.

   g Nat smokes his last ....

After you read

21 Are you more afraid of birds now? Will you look at them differently when you put this book down? Do you want to see Alfred Hitchcock's film of 'The Birds'?

Writing

22 The story stops but it doesn't end. What will happen? Write the end of the story.

23 You get away from England in a ship. The ship takes you to America. You saw the bird attacks before you left. They are all over the country. Write a story for a newspaper in New York.

24 After the children are asleep, Nat tells his wife about Mr and Mrs Trigg and Jim, the farm boy. His wife asks a lot of questions. Write the conversation.

25 A different animal starts to attack people in their homes. This time it happens in your country. Write a story.

26 You are making a new film of *The Birds* in your country. Where will you film it? Who will play Nat, Nat's wife and Mr and Mrs Trigg? Write about it.

27 The next night the birds leave. They don't come back. People slowly start to live their lives again. Nat's wife writes to her sister. She tells her about the attacks. Write her letter.

28 Do you have a bird at home? Do you have other animals? How do you look after them? What must you do for them?

29 Write about *The Birds* for a friend. Did you like it? Will your friend like it?

Answers for the Activities in this book are available from the Penguin Readers website. A free Activity Worksheet is also available from the website. Activity Worksheets are part of the Penguin Teacher Support Programme, which also includes Progress Tests and Graded Reader Guidelines. For more information, please visit:
www.penguinreaders.com.

WORD LIST *with example sentences*

attack (v/n) Two men *attacked* him in the street and took his money.

beak (v) The bird had some food in its *beak*.

blood (n) He killed the bird and then washed its *blood* from his hands.

bloody (adj) His hands were *bloody* after he killed the bird.

crowd (n/v) It was an important game, and there was a big *crowd* – about 10,000 people.

farm (n) I live on a *farm*. My father is a *farmer*, so we have a lot of animals.

God (n) *God* is important for Christians, Jews and Muslims.

hunting (adj) *Hunting* birds kill and eat smaller birds and animals.

line (n) A long *line* of people waited for the shop to open.
  We can't use the telephone because the phone *line* is down.

must (v) We haven't got any food, so we *must* buy some.

news (n) I listen to the *news* on the radio and read a newspaper every morning.

peck (v) I tried to give some food to the bird, but it *pecked* my hand.

roof (n) The rain fell noisily on the *roof* of the house.

scratching (n/v) What's that *scratching* noise on the door? It's the cat. It wants to come in.

scream (n/v) She fell from the window, and we heard a loud *scream*.

seagull (n) Those grey and white birds are *seagulls*.

thank (v) He gave me some money and I *thanked* him.

tin (n) Food in *tins* stays OK for years.

together (adv) They are good friends, so they often do things *together*.

wing (n) Birds and aeroplanes have *wings*.

Pirates of the Caribbean
The Curse of the Black Pearl

Elizabeth lives on a Caribbean island, a very dangerous place.
A young blacksmith is interested in her, but pirates are interested
too. Where do the pirates come from and what do they want? Is
there really a curse on their ship? And why can't they enjoy their
gold?

Moby Dick
Herman Melville

Moby Dick is the most dangerous whale in the oceans. Captain
Ahab fought him and lost a leg. Now he hates Moby Dick. He
wants to kill him. But can Captain Ahab and his men find the
great white whale? A young sailor, Ishmael, tells the story of their
exciting and dangerous trip.

Jaws

Amity is a quiet town near New York. One night a woman goes for
a swim in the sea. The next morning somebody finds her body on
the beach. Brody is the Amity policeman. He thinks there's a killer
shark out there. But the important people don't listen to him.

*There are hundreds of Penguin Readers to choose from – world classics,
film adaptations, modern-day crime and adventure, short stories,
biographies, American classics, non-fiction, plays ...*

For a complete list of all Penguin Readers titles, please contact your local
Pearson Longman office or visit our website.

www.penguinreaders.com

PENGUIN READERS *recommends*

The Lady in the Lake
Raymond Chandler

Detective Philip Marlowe is looking for Derace Kingsley's wife, Crystal. Is she dead or not? Marlowe finds more than one dead body and learns about women, drugs, men in love, and a police cover-up. Who killed *The Lady in the Lake* and why?

A Christmas Carol
Charles Dickens

Scrooge is a cold, hard man. He loves money, and he doesn't like people. He really doesn't like Christmas. But then some ghosts visit him. They show him his past life, his life now, and a possible future. Will Scrooge learn from the ghosts? Can he change?

Kidnapped
Robert Louis Stevenson

After his parents die, young David Balfour goes to the house of his uncle Ebenezer. But his uncle is a dangerous man. When he puts David on a ship to America, a difficult and dangerous time begins. But who is the stranger on the ship? Can he help David?

There are hundreds of Penguin Readers to choose from – world classics, film adaptations, modern-day crime and adventure, short stories, biographies, American classics, non-fiction, plays ...

For a complete list of all Penguin Readers titles, please contact your local Pearson Longman office or visit our website.

www.penguinreaders.com

Longman Dictionaries

Express yourself with confidence!

Longman has led the way in ELT dictionaries since 1935. We constantly talk to students and teachers around the world to find out what they need from a learner's dictionary.

Why choose a Longman dictionary?

Easy to understand

Longman invented the Defining Vocabulary – 2000 of the most common words which are used to write the definitions in our dictionaries. So Longman definitions are always clear and easy to understand.

Real, natural English

All Longman dictionaries contain natural examples taken from real-life that help explain the meaning of a word and show you how to use it in context.

Avoid common mistakes

Longman dictionaries are written specially for learners, and we make sure that you get all the help you need to avoid common mistakes. We analyse typical learners' mistakes and include notes on how to avoid them.

Innovative CD-ROMs

Longman are leaders in dictionary CD-ROM innovation. Did you know that a dictionary CD-ROM includes features to help improve your pronunciation, help you practice for exams and improve your writing skills?

For details of all Longman dictionaries, and to choose the one that's right for you, visit our website:

www.longman.com/dictionaries